ment

averse Islands

NANABIJOU (SLEEPING GIANT)

Gitchee Gumee
(Lake Superior)

Winnipeg

C A N A D A

Montreal

Minneapolis

Toronto

U S A

Detroit

Chicago

New York

ISLE ROYALE

The Red Sash

Groundwood Books / House of Anansi Press
110 Spadina Avenue, Suite 801, Toronto, Ontario M5V 2K4
Distributed in the USA by Publishers Group West
1700 Fourth Street, Berkeley, CA 94710

We acknowledge for their financial support of our publishing
program the Canada Council for the Arts, the Government of
Canada through the Book Publishing Industry Development
Program (BPIDP) and the Ontario Arts Council.

ONTARIO ARTS COUNCIL
CONSEIL DES ARTS DE L'ONTARIO

Library and Archives Canada Cataloging in Publication

Pendziwol, Jean E.
The red sash / Jean E. Pendziwol ; pictures by Nicolas Debon.

ISBN 0-88899-589-X

1. Métis—Juvenile fiction. 2. Fur traders—Juvenile fiction.

I. Debon, Nicolas   II. Title.

PS8581.E55312R43 2005   jC813'.54   C2005-900657-9

Design by Michael Solomon
Printed and bound in China

The illustrations were done in gouache and mixed media on
cold-press watercolor paper.

To my favorite voyageur,
Colin — J E P

To Aidan, Élina, Marianne
and Fabrice — N D

The Red Sash

Jean E. Pendziwol

PICTURES BY

Nicolas Debon

A Groundwood Book
House of Anansi Press

TORONTO BERKELEY

THE SUN is rising over Nanabijou who lies sleeping on the great sea Gitchee Gumee. My sister Isabelle and I wake up. I can see Mother through the entrance of our wigwam. She and Grandmother are cooking our breakfast over the fire, and the smell is making my stomach rumble with hunger. Isabelle and I dress quickly, careful not to wake the baby who is still asleep on a warm bear hide.

Across the river, at Fort William, I see the smoke from many small fires rising above the canvas tents of the voyageurs. It is the time of rendezvous, when winter traders paddle to Fort William with their packs of furs to meet the North West Company canoes coming from Montreal bringing supplies. Around the campfires, the voyageurs trade stories about storms and fog on the big lakes, about portages and bears and racing across Lake Winnipeg.

Mother and I push our canoe into the water to cross the Kaministiquia River. I am not strong enough to carry two packs over a portage, but I am strong enough to help my mother paddle our canoe. Someday, I will carry three packs over the Mountain Portage at Kakabeka Falls, and I will have many stories to tell when I come to rendezvous.

But today we will work at Fort William.

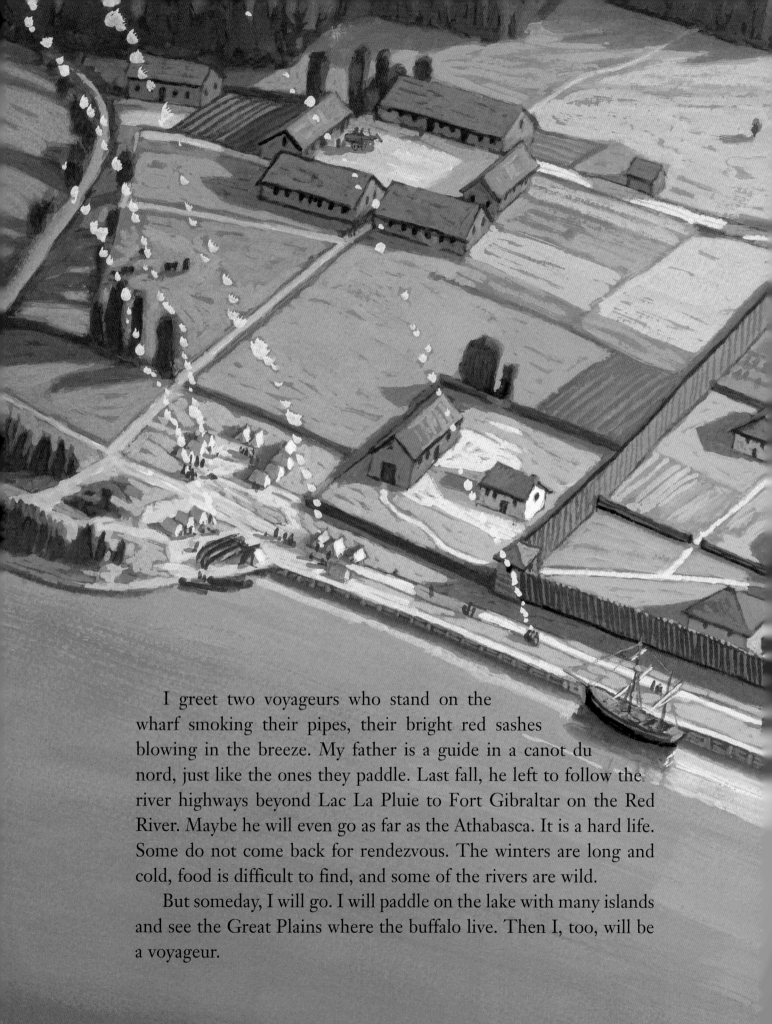

I greet two voyageurs who stand on the wharf smoking their pipes, their bright red sashes blowing in the breeze. My father is a guide in a canot du nord, just like the ones they paddle. Last fall, he left to follow the river highways beyond Lac La Pluie to Fort Gibraltar on the Red River. Maybe he will even go as far as the Athabasca. It is a hard life. Some do not come back for rendezvous. The winters are long and cold, food is difficult to find, and some of the rivers are wild.

But someday, I will go. I will paddle on the lake with many islands and see the Great Plains where the buffalo live. Then I, too, will be a voyageur.

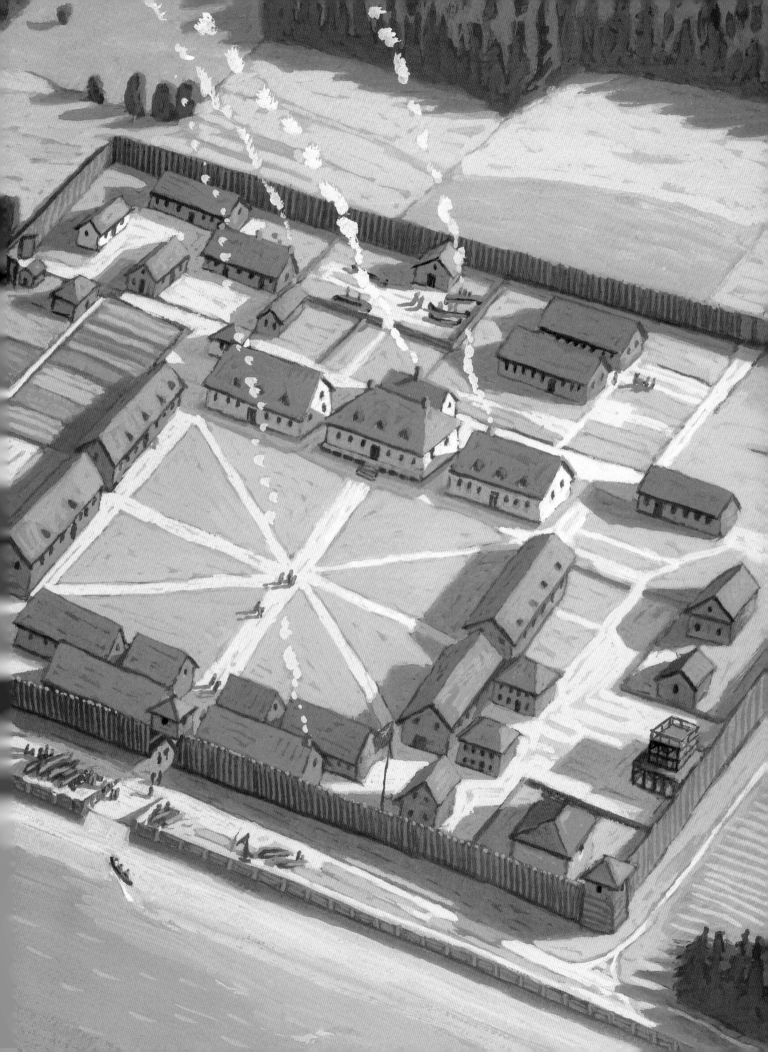

All around us, the fort is waking up. In the bakery, bread is rising and the oven is hot. Mother helps in the kitchen, and she sets the baby's tikinaagan down where she can see it. Isabelle works in the dairy. I go to look for eggs at the farm.

The rooster struts about on the gate to the pig pen, boasting in a loud voice. Inside the barn, the hens scratch for cracked corn on the ground. I fill a large makuk with eggs and carry it to the kitchen. Isabelle is there, too, with butter and fresh buttermilk for the busy cook and his helpers. There will be a feast tonight in the Great Hall as more and more gentlemen arrive for rendezvous. Maybe my father will arrive today, too.

The blacksmith's hammer bangs against the anvil, and I can smell the sweet scent of freshly cut wood as the carpenter cuts a log for the palisade wall. Some of the voyageurs are helping him.

"Would you like to go to the islands?" asks John as Isabelle and I stop for a drink at the well. John is the doctor's son, and he is older than I am. He is looking at me, but I think he is asking Isabelle.

There are hare on the Traverse Islands. It has been a long time since Grandmother has cooked hare.

We push our canoe into the river and paddle out onto the great sea. It is not far. I pretend that I am a voyageur and paddle hard to a little bay on the largest island. We lift our canoe out of the water and gently place it on the rocky beach. I go to set my snares on the furthest side of the island.

The scent of warm earth and pine fills the air as I explore the woods and climb the great cliffs. From here, I can see across the big bay. A brigade of canoes from Montreal is nearing the feet of Nanabijou. I wait and watch. The canoes are coming closer — the voyageurs are paddling hard.

Behind me, the sky has grown dark. Black clouds boil up with eerie green beneath them. I can feel the storm coming long before it touches the waters of the lake.

I quickly check my snares and find a fat brown hare! Scrambling down the cliff to the beach, I look for Isabelle and John. I cannot see them.

Just then, the storm hits. The trees behind me moan and groan in loud, angry voices. The wind pushes them until their trunks bend and snap. I find shelter among the boulders along the shore.

Out on the lake, the waters are churning to foam. The icy green waves hurry and tumble over each other not knowing which way to go. I can see them crashing against the rocks of the point with a surge of white spray. Rain is falling but I can hardly feel it, for the wind has caught the waves, picking them up and dropping them over me until all my clothes are soaked.

I stumble over the boulders around the island. From here, I can see the voyageurs' canoes. They are much closer now. These men are not singing. They are paddling hard to get to the shelter of the island. In the middle of one canoe sits a gentleman, holding onto his beaver felt hat.

I scramble along the slippery shore and wade out into the water, hoping to catch the bow of the first canoe. But I lose my footing and fall. The water is so cold! When I get back on my feet, the gentleman's canoe is nearly on top of me, so I grab the bow and steady it. It is almost full of water. The voyageurs jump out and lift the gentleman ashore. I can see now that the birch bark bottom is torn.

The other canoes are waiting off shore. They are piled with packs holding blankets, beads, trinkets, pots and tobacco to trade with the Indians for furs. It is too rocky for the canoes to come ashore here, and the squall is already easing. They will continue on to Fort William. But the gentleman's canoe cannot go any further today.

"'Well, you are a fine young voyageur," says the gentleman. He has a strong Scottish accent. "I would sign you on, but it seems I am without a canoe!"

I almost smile. Just then, Isabelle and John arrive. They have been looking for me.

I stand up straight and tall, ignoring the wind and wet. "We have a canoe," I say. "It is across the island in the shelter of the bay. We can paddle you to Fort William."

The wind is calmer and the rain has stopped. It has been a long journey for the gentleman and Fort William is so close.

I sit in the bow of the canoe with the hare lying at my feet. My red paddle is flashing as it dips in and out of the sparkling blue water. The gentleman sits in the middle, and the North West Company flag is flying. John and Isabelle paddle, too. The waves are still large, and we have to work hard to reach the mouth of the river. As we approach, we begin to sing, "En roulant ma boule roulant! En roulant ma boule!" Cannon fire announces our arrival and bagpipes play in greeting.

But before we reach the wharf, I hear an echo of our song. "Roulis-roulant ma boule roulant! En roulant ma boule roulant! En roulant ma boule!"

And then voyageurs whoop and cheer as they turn the bend of the river, red paddles flashing as they dip in and out of the sparkling blue water. There are six canoes from the North, and I see my father sitting in one of them!

A crowd has gathered to greet the canoes. Mother is there. Father smiles at her, and then looks at me and Isabelle sitting in the canoe with the gentleman. I will have a good story to tell around the campfire tonight. But first I help them to unload the packs of furs that have traveled from deep in the wilds of the Indian territories – wolf, muskrat, deer, fox, buffalo, mink… but most important, beaver. I can only carry one pack at a time.

Father has gifts for us all. There is ribbon for the baby's tikinaagan, an ivory comb for Mother, and for Isabelle, a fabric pouch filled with colorful beads. Father turns to me, and I wait eagerly.

"You have grown, my little voyageur," he says. "It looks like you will be needing this sooner than I expected."

My father hands me a bright red sash, the sash of a voyageur.

It is dark, but no one at the fort is sleeping. Inside the Great Hall, the women have joined the men. The fiddler is playing a reel, and the elegantly dressed gentlemen dance with the girls of the fort. Mother and Father are dancing, too.

Isabelle and John are dancing in the square. The voyageurs dance along with them. They are telling stories about cold winters and wild animals, long portages and turbulent rapids. They are wrestling and playing games. They are happy to be here after such a long winter, after paddling many hard days. They are happy to celebrate rendezvous!

My bright red sash blows in the breeze. I begin to dance, too.

Fort William, on Lake Superior, was the inland headquarters of the North West Company from 1803 to 1821, when the company merged with the Hudson's Bay Company.

Explorers such as Alexander Mackenzie, David Thompson and Simon Fraser were North West Company wintering partners. Their explorations helped to open up trade routes throughout the interior "Indian Territories" as far as the Pacific and Arctic Oceans. Partners spent the winter at posts in the interior, organizing trade with the native people who exchanged furs for goods including blankets and linens, arms and ammunition, pots and kettles, liquor and tobacco.

The North West Company's main headquarters was in Montreal, where furs were prepared for shipment to London, England. Since it was too far to take furs from the far northwest to Montreal and return to the trading posts in one ice-free season, the traders or voyageurs, in brigades of canots du nord, would bring these furs as far as Fort William. Meanwhile, brigades of large canoes from Montreal carried goods and supplies to Fort William for distribution to posts in the interior. These canoes then carried the furs back to Montreal and from there they were shipped overseas.

Agents or directors of the company, like William McGillivray, also came up to Fort William from Montreal to meet with the wintering partners. They would discuss business, trade and the increasing competition from the Hudson's Bay Company. This gathering of traders and voyageurs from East and West at Fort William each summer was called rendezvous.

Many of the North West Company partners, clerks, tradesmen and voyageurs took native wives according to "the custom of the country." These fur trade marriages strengthened ties between traders and native bands. Their Métis or "mixed blood" children played an important role in the fur trade, working as interpreters, guides and clerks, and a few became partners. The women sewed moccasins, hunted and fished, worked on the fort's farm, and helped make the many birch bark canoes needed in the fur trade. Without them, the fur trade would not have existed.

Glossary

boule (En roulant ma boule roulant...): Voyageurs often sang songs while paddling in order to pass the time and to keep a steady rhythm. This particular one is a nonsense song about rolling balls and was usually sung in a round.

canot du nord: A north canoe. Only 24 feet (7 m) long and paddled by five voyageurs, it was smaller and more easily portaged than the 36-foot (11 m) Montreal canoe.

Gitchee Gumee: The Ojibwa name for Lake Superior meaning "Great Water."

makuk: A container made out of birch bark, sewn together with spruce root.

Nanabijou: A peninsula in Thunder Bay, now called the Sleeping Giant. According to legend, Nanabijou was the Ojibwa spirit of deep sea waters.

tikinaagan: A baby carrier, sometimes called a cradle board.

Traverse Islands: A group of four islands in Thunder Bay, now called the Welcome Islands.

voyageurs: The men who worked in the fur trade and traveled by canoe.

FORT WILLIAM

AND ITS SURROUNDINGS

DURING THE TIME OF THE

NORTH WEST COMPANY

(c. 1803-1821)

5 mi.

5 km.

Site of
present-day
Thunder Bay

Kakabeka Falls
(Mountain
Portage)

Kaministiquia River

Fort Willi

Native e